Parrot Park

MARY MURPHY

ILLUSTRATED BY
JESSICA AHLBERG

WALKER
BOOKS

For my father, Seán Murphy
M.M.

For everybody at Stewart Headlam Primary School
J.A.

This is a work of fiction. Names, characters, places and incidents
either are the product of the author's imagination or, if real, are used
fictitiously. All statements, activities, stunts, descriptions, information
and material of any other kind contained herein are included for
entertainment purposes only and should not be relied on for
accuracy or replicated as they may result in injury.

First published 2006 by Walker Books Ltd
87 Vauxhall Walk, London SE11 5HJ

2 4 6 8 10 9 7 5 3

Text © 2006 Mary Murphy
Illustrations © 2006 Jessica Ahlberg

The right of Mary Murphy and Jessica Ahlberg to be identified as author
and illustrator respectively of this work has been asserted by them in
accordance with the Copyright, Designs and Patents Act 1988

This book has been typeset in Bembo Educational
and Myriad Tilt Bold

Printed and bound in China

British Library Cataloguing in Publication Data:
a catalogue record for this book is available from the British Library

ISBN 978-1-4063-0195-3

www.walker.co.uk

Grass
7

Scratch
25

Aliens
45

All the Murphys live at
53 Parrot Park: Mammy, Daddy
and six children like stairs.

Rory is nine,
the eldest.
He knows
everything,
nearly.

Anna is seven.
She wants to be a boy.

Mary is six.
She wants to be
a vet in Africa.

The twins are four.
Catherine is the ballerina.
Cormac is wild, wild, wild.

Susan is only one. She smiles and listens to nobody.

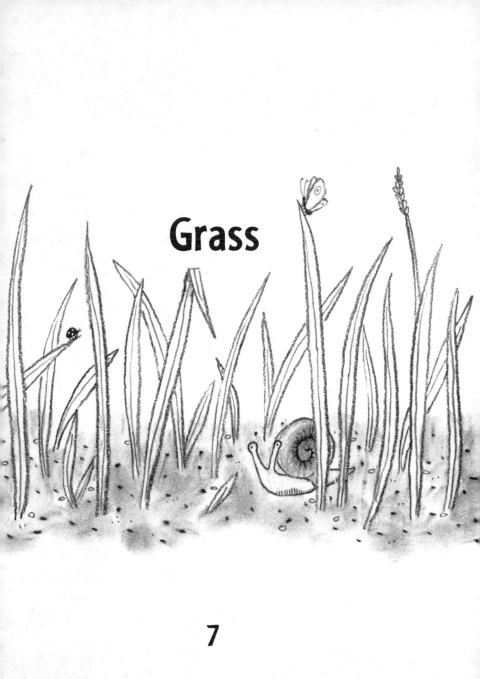

Grass

All over Dublin the grass grows tall and pale in the long hot summer.

At 53 Parrot Park it is higher than Rory's knees, and as high as Catherine's shorts.

"Time to cut it," says Daddy.

Daddy and Mammy and Susan
go indoors. All the other Murphys
search the garden for things that
could break the lawnmower,
or that the lawnmower could break.

"We have to find three things each,"
says Rory.

"At least," says Anna.

The top of the grass is scratchy,
pale and dry. Lower down is cool,
dark and soft.

"I've found five things," says Cormac.
He has two stones, one with a hole
in it, a straight stick, a tennis ball and a
sock. He found them too quickly.

"We found these last time," says Rory.

"I remember that stick," says Mary.

"You hid them," says Catherine.

Last time the grass was cut, Cormac hid these things in the coal shed so he wouldn't have to search this time.

Now he has to find three more things.

Rory collects stones
from Smarty's hiding place.

Anna finds her book, fat after last
week's rain. She reads it, still searching,
and trips on a cup. Now she has found
two things.

"I thought you were lost for ever!" says Mary when she finds Teeny Teddy. There are snails beside him and she collects them.

Catherine finds a bright bracelet. "I hope I can keep it," she says.

Cormac finds a stick and breaks it into three pieces.

Everything is put on the step.
Smarty's stones. Sticks that Pookie
has chased but not found. The snails.
Lego from a game of soldiers. The cup.
Catherine's bracelet, Anna's book,
Teeny Teddy and the five things
Cormac has kept from last time.

Now Daddy Murphy pushes
the lawnmower out of the garage.

He pulls the cord. The mower spits
and snarls. Daddy snarls back, until
RARARARAAAAAA! goes the mower.

Then Daddy cuts the grass.

Daddy Murphy does not cut grass in straight lines. No. He cuts in a maze. Up and across and wiggle, and when it is an interesting and difficult maze all the Murphys play Crazy Maze.

Catherine stuffs
grass down Cormac's
back. It scrapes,
Cormac squeals,
Anna jumps on
Catherine, and Daddy
whistles like a referee.

Everyone freezes.

"Time to finish the grass,"
says Daddy.

He cuts the between
bits of the maze.

All the Murphys collect the grass in
a big heap. They are green-skinned,
stained all over from grass.

"Good work, Martians," says Daddy.

Rory throws the tennis ball:
up, catch, up, catch, up ...
over the wall.

Catherine takes her bracelet
and Anna takes her book.
Daddy picks up the sock.

The snails slide out of the sun.

Soon Smarty sneaks away

with a stone.

The found things

are disappearing.

All the Murphys scratch where grass sneaked into their clothes, and sniff the delicious smell of cut summer grass, and look. Their garden is just like any garden now, with short, smart grass.

But although they can't see it, the grass is silently growing – just like all the Murphys.

Scratch

*S*cratch. *Scritch-scratch. Itch-itch-itch-itch.*

"Stop scratching, Cormac,"
says Mammy.

"I can't help it," says Cormac.

Neither can Anna nor Mary. They
bury fingers in their hair, scrabbling
with short fingernails.

Catherine scratches.

"You're making me itchy," says Rory. *Scratch*. Susan doesn't scratch, but she will when she wakes.

"Oh no," groans Mammy. "Lice. How did that happen? Last time was when Anna used someone else's hairbrush."

"I used Linda's hairbrush yesterday,"
says Catherine.

"Ah," says Mammy.

"I want long blonde hair like Linda,"
says Catherine.

"Well now you have lice like Linda,"
says Cormac.

But the lice are
not from Linda.

"I've been itchy
since my Scout
trip," says Rory.

"A week!" says
Mammy. "Why didn't
you tell me?"

"Because last time you
killed all the lice," says
Rory. "Don't kill them
this time, Mammy!"

"Don't kill them,
Mammy, don't,"
say all the Murphys.
Scratch-atch-atch.

30

"Say if we all have
a hundred lice, that's six
hundred between us," says
Rory. "You can't just kill
six hundred animals."

"Sorry," says Mammy.
"They're going."

"We'd have the most pets
of anyone in Ireland," says
Mary. *Itchy-scritchy-scratch*.

"They're not pets," says
Mammy firmly.

"They're wild animals!" says
Anna. *Scritch-itch-scratch*.

"They're driving you
wild," says Mammy.

31

Susan wakes and starts rubbing her head.

"All the Murphys: outside," orders Mammy. "I'll get the bathroom ready."

All the Murphys go into their front garden. Mr Lahart is in his garden trimming his perfect hedge.

"We have lice," says Catherine.

"All of us," says Rory. "About six hundred between us."

"Imagine," says Mr Lahart. "They must think they are on foresty planets." He pats his shiny head. "Not like if they were on my head."

"WE HAVE LICE!" Cormac shouts to Karl Jones.

"ALL OF US!" shouts Rory.

"ABOUT …"

"… SIX HUNDRED BETWEEN US!" shout all the Murphys.

"Six hundred what?" asks
Mrs Miller.

"Lice," say all the Murphys.

"Oh," says Mrs Miller,
and walks quickly home.

"Let's shake our hair and set the lice free," says Mary. So all the Murphys shake their heads and dance and tumble head over heels.

Catherine
shakes her hair
into a rose bush
so the lice can live
somewhere nice.
Anna climbs
the tree to shake
her hair.

They are dizzy by the time Mammy
comes out.

"Ready," she says. "Let's get started."

All the Murphys go inside.

There is a knock on the door.

It is Mrs Jones with an
electric comb that zaps nits.

Behind her is Mr Lahart with a
newspaper cutting. It says if you use
hair conditioner the lice go to sleep
and you can comb them out.

"Thank you!" says Mammy.
"I'll try anything."

Behind Mr Lahart is Anne Miller.

"My Mammy says I'm not allowed to play with all the Murphys because you have lice," says Anne Miller, and she runs away. Cormac chases, shaking his hair at her.

"Lice! Lice! I'm going to give you lice!"

Anne Miller speeds up and swings
the gate to block Cormac.

"Anne Miller certainly is
a good runner," says
Rory calmly.

"Get right back here, Cormac!"
calls Mammy. "You're first."

Everyone lines up. Mammy
opens the Lice Killer shampoo.
She opens a bottle of
hair conditioner.

The electric comb is
downstairs for later.

"Close your eyes
and mouth and put
your head back,"
says Mammy.

Fifty-three Parrot Park smells like
a chemical plant. The pillowcases and
sheets and all the towels have to be
washed.

Poor Mammy.

But at least all
the Murphys
have stopped
scratching.
For now.

Aliens

It is autumn all over the Phoenix Park,
all over Dublin, all over the windy
country. Leaves fly. Birds gang in the sky.
Acroplanes trail long, thin lines.
Catherine finds the biggest conker.
How come it ends up in Cormac's pocket?

After the park all the Murphys visit
Granny and Grandad, who live near by.
Granny makes chips and sausages.

Then all the Murphys play Monsters
in the shadowy hall. Except Susan –
Monsters is a scary game
for babies.

THE RULES

One Murphy is the monster.

You have to get from Granny's bedroom, at one end of the hall, past three more doors to the spare room at the other end.

When the monster catches you, you are a slave Slaves hide behind doors to capture innocent Murphys.

Another monster slave!

The river is dark blue at the end of
Granny's garden, and so is the sky.

It is time to go home.

The road home is by the high
park wall.

The car is squashed full of
grumpy Murphys.

Rory says, "I see a flying saucer!"

Anna sees it too, drifting behind
the trees.

"It landed in the park,"
says Rory.

"What is it like?" asks Mammy.

"Big slow lights," says Rory,
"going behind the trees."

"Yes," says Anna. "Big lights going
slowly into the wood."

"I saw it first," says Cormac.

"I did," say Rory and Anna and
Mary and Catherine.

"We'd better find it," says Rory.

"There could be aliens," says Anna.

So Daddy drives in the next park gate.

Now the car is squashed
full of serious Murphys.

The dark hills bulge.

The car lights nose along the
black shifting road.

"Dark," says Susan.

"Light!" says Cormac.

Closer... It is the park-keeper's house.

The park-keeper's dog charges and
roars at the car.

In the daytime he is a friendly fellow.
Now his eyes flash red and yellow.

Smarty and Pookie bark like drums.

The car sneaks on.

"This is where we were today," says Mammy.

It looks completely different now.

"I think the flying saucer is around here," says Rory.

Daddy stops the car. He turns off the lights.

Black. Silent.

Mammy opens her window. Night creeps in, smelling leafy.

58

Slowly all the
Murphys start to see.
Stars ping into the
sky; tree shapes appear.

Slowly they start to hear:
tiny rustles and sighs.

Tiny lights blink on
and off around the car,
like eyes.

"Aliens," whispers Rory. Eyes with
shadowy
bodies. They
watch all the
Murphys.
All the Murphys
watch them.

"Not aliens," says Mammy. "Deer."
Deer watch all the Murphys, and all
the Murphys watch them.
"We're the aliens," says Daddy.

The deer blink their huge eyes.

   All the Murphys hear them breathe,
and hear themselves breathe.

   All the Murphys feel the same.
Maybe the deer do too.

"I'd say the flying saucer is gone,"
says Daddy.

He turns on the car lights and the
deer back away, ears twitching. Off
creeps the car, further into the park.

They see more deer, and *swoosh!*
a bird. But a flying saucer? No.

The car goes out
the park gate.

"We could
be invaded by
aliens," says Rory.
"They might be
nice," says Mammy.
"Nicer than you,"
says Cormac, pinching
Catherine.
"Ouch!" yelps Catherine.
Cormac pokes Mary.
"Nicer than you!"
Mary pokes him back. "Or you!"
All the Murphys push and poke,
going, "Nicer than you! Nicer
than YOU!"
Except Susan, fast asleep.

Back at Parrot Park all the Murphys
have a story from Daddy. It is about
people from another planet.

In fact they are very nice,
really nice, quite like
all the Murphys.